THE THIRD MAN

Karin Hüber II HH2

GRAHAM GREENE

THE THIRD MAN

EASY READERS

ER

EASY READERS

The vocabulary is based on
Salling/Hvid: English-Danish Basic Dictionary
Weis: Grund- und Aufbauwortschatz, Englisch
Thorndike: The Teacher's Word Book
West: A General Service List

EDITORS
Aage Salling
Erik Hvid *Denmark*

ADVISERS
Marja Wuorenheimo *Finland*
Otto Weise *Germany*
G. de Groot *The Netherlands*
Erling Rundstrøm *Norway*
Brita af Ekenstam *Sweden*

Cover design: Ib Jørgensen
Illustrations: Oskar Jørgensen

ISBN Denmark 87-429-7451-8

Printed in Denmark by
Grafisk Institut A/S, Copenhagen

GRAHAM GREENE
(1904–)

was born at Berkhamsted in Hertfordshire, where his father was a headmaster. He is one of the greatest British prose writers of today. His capacity for narrative recalls that of R. L. Stevenson, his father's cousin, but he never writes a story for its own sake; over and above the plot something else happens which is of far greater importance than the events which make up the plot. He wants to show how inevitably and mercilessly the choice between good and evil comes into the life of every man. Flight is often the theme he chooses to deprive his characters of everything which can obscure this issue, and with deep psychological insight Greene shows us the result in persons of different turns of mind. His style is clear, his symbols well chosen, and his language carefully phrased to express exactly what he wants to say.

Other Books by Graham Greene:

The Man Within (1929), Journey Without Maps (1936), A Gun for Sale (1936), Brighton Rock (1938), The Power and the Glory (1940), The Heart of the Matter (1948), The End of the Affair (1951), The Quiet American (1955), The Comedians (1966).

I

I saw Rollo Martins first at Harry Lime's *funeral.* It was February, and the *grave-diggers* had been forced to use electric *drills* to open the frozen ground in Vienna's Central *Cemetery.* It was as if nature were doing its best to *reject* Lime, but we got him in at last and laid the earth back on him like *bricks,* and Rollo Martins walked away as though his long legs wanted to break into a run, and the tears of a boy ran down his thirty-five-year-old face.

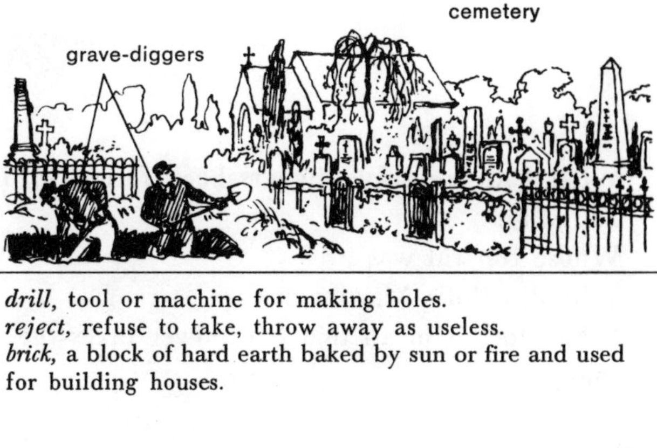

drill, tool or machine for making holes.
reject, refuse to take, throw away as useless.
brick, a block of hard earth baked by sun or fire and used for building houses.

Rollo Martins believed in friendship, and that was why what happened later was a worse shock to him than it would have been to you or me.

If you are to understand this sad and strange story, you must have an idea at least of the background – the city of Vienna, divided up in zones among the four powers; the Russian, the British, the American, the French zones, and in the centre of the city the *Inner Stadt* under the control of all four Powers. In this Inner Stadt each power in turn, for a month at a time, takes, as we call it, "the chair", and takes care of things. I never knew Vienna between the wars, and I am too young to remember the old Vienna with its Strauss music and its easy charm; to me it is simply a city of ruins which turned that February into blocks of snow and ice.

Questions

1. What had the grave-diggers been forced to do? and why?
2. Whose funeral was it?
3. Why did Rollo Martins cry?
4. What does it mean that one power takes the chair?

2

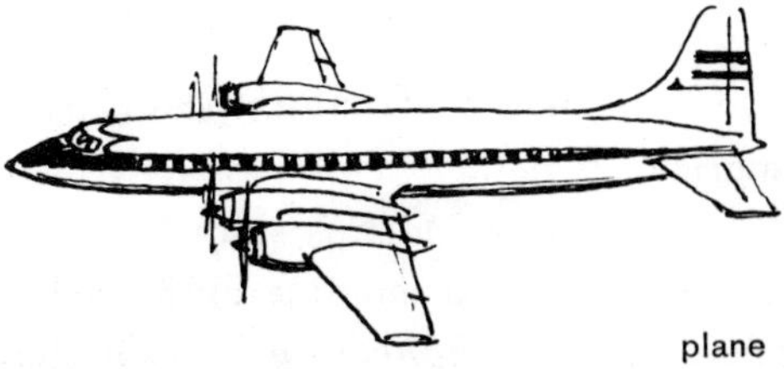
plane

A British subject can still travel – if he takes with him only five pounds, which he is forbidden to spend abroad, but if Rollo Martins had not received an invitation from Lime he would not have been allowed to enter Austria.

Lime had suggested that Martins should write something about Vienna and had promised to pay his expenses. Though this was not Martins' *line* he had agreed to do so. His usual line was the writing of cheap *Westerns* under the name of B. Dexter. He had many readers but a small income.

A strange thing had happened at Frankfurt, where the *plane* from London stopped for an hour. Martins was sitting in the American *canteen* when a man he could recognize from twenty feet away as a journalist came up to his table.

"You Mr. Dexter?" he asked.

"Yes," Martins said.

"Would you like to say something? I represent the American newspaper here. We'd like to know what you think of Frankfurt."

"I only touched down ten minutes ago."

---

line, kind of work.
western, story about men and Red Indians in the Wild West.
canteen, a place where food and drinks are sold to soldiers. (here: to travellers).

"All right," the man said. "What about your views on the American *novel?*"

"I don't read them," Martins said.

The man pointed at a small grey-haired man at another table. "*Do you happen to know* if that's Carey?"

"No. What Carey?"

"J. G. Carey, of course."

"I've never heard of him."

"You *novelists* live out of the world." The man walked across the room to meet the great Carey, but Martins could not help feeling proud that the other had spoken of him as a novelist, and that carried him over the *disappointment* when Lime was not there to meet him at the *airport.*

Nor was there any Lime to meet him at the Hotel Astoria, where the bus landed him, nor any message – only one from someone he had never heard of called Crabbin. "We expected you on tomorrow's plane. Please stay where you are. Coming round. Hotel room *booked.*" But Rollo Martins was not the kind of man who stayed around. If you stayed in a hotel, sooner or later something happened, and Rollo Martins wanted none of that.

---

novel, long story that takes up a whole book.
novelist, person who writes such stories.
do you happen to know, do you know by chance.
disappointment, feeling of sadness that something expected did not happen.
airport, place near a big town where aeroplanes take off and land.
booked, reserved.

He had been given Lime's address and he was not very eager to meet the man called Crabbin; a mistake must have been made. So Martins drove straight away to the building in the British zone. He kept the taxi waiting while he went up to the third floor.

Martins hadn't got to the second floor before he knew that he would not find Lime there – it was as if he would not find Lime anywhere in Vienna, and, as he reached the third floor and saw the big black *bow* over the door *handle*, anywhere in the world at all.

Of course it might be a cook who had died, a *housekeeper*, anybody but Harry Lime, but he knew – he felt he had known twenty stairs down – that Lime, the Lime he had looked up to now for twenty years, since their first meeting in a school corridor, was gone. Martins wasn't wrong. After he had rung the bell half a dozen times a small man put his head out from another flat and told him, "It's no use. There's nobody there. He's dead."

"Herr Lime?"

"Herr Lime, of course."

Martins said to me later, "At first it didn't mean a thing. It was just a bit of information, like what

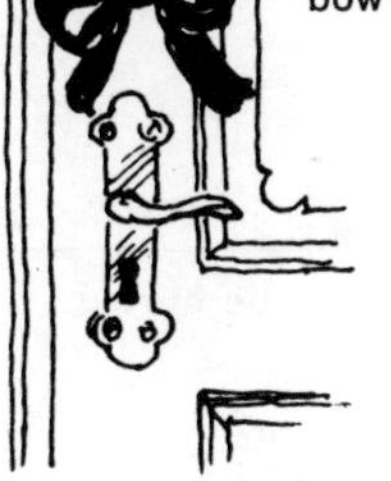

---

housekeeper, woman taking care of a house.

you see in a newspaper. I said to him, 'When did it happen? How?'"

"He was run over by a car," the man said. "Last Thursday." And then, as if it were really none of his business, "They're burying him this afternoon. You've just missed them."

"Them?"

"Oh, a couple of friends and the *coffin.*"

"Wasn't he in hospital?"

"There was no sense in taking him to hospital. He was killed on his own doorstep. The car struck him on his shoulder and *bowled* him *over* like a *rabbit.*"

"Where are they burying him?" he asked the stranger.

"In the Central Cemetery. They'll have a hard time of it in this frost."

He had no idea how to pay for his taxi, or indeed where in Vienna he could find a room in which he could live for five English pounds, but that problem had to be put off until he had seen the last of Harry Lime. He drove straight out of town into the British zone where the Central Cemetery lay. One passed through the Russian zone to reach it, and took a short

rabbit

---

coffin, box in which a dead body is placed to be buried.
bowl over, knock over, run down.

cut through the American zone. The trams ran along the high wall of the cemetery, and for a mile on the other side was the endless line of *gravestones*.

It was just chance that he reached the funeral in time. A small group was gathered, a priest had just spoken, his words coming through the snow, and a coffin was on the point of being lowered into the ground. Two men stood at the grave; one carried some flowers that he seemed to have forgotten to drop on the coffin, for the other man touched his elbow, so that he dropped them with a start. A girl stood a little way away with her hands over her face, and I stood twenty yards away by another grave – just a man in a *mackintosh* I was to Martins. He came up to me and said, "Could you tell me who they are burying?"

"A fellow called Lime," I said, and was surprised to see the tears start to this stranger's eyes; he did not look like a man who wept.

Martins stood there, till the end, close beside me. As soon as the affair was over he walked away on his long legs, back to his taxi. He did not try to speak to anyone, and the tears were now really running, at any rate the few drops that can come up in the eyes of a man at our age.

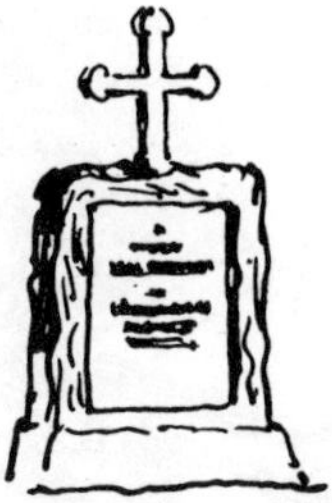

gravestone

---

mackintosh, raincoat.

I followed Martins. I knew the other three. I wanted to know the stranger. I caught him up by his taxi and said, "I haven't any transport. Would you give me a *lift* into town?"

"Of course," he said. I knew the driver of my *jeep* would see me as we came out and follow us. As we drove away I noticed that he never looked behind.

I said, "My name is Calloway."

"Martins," he said.

"You were a friend of Lime?"

"Yes." Most people in the last week would have *hesitated* before saying so much.

"Been here long?"

"I only came this afternoon from England. Harry had asked me to stay with him. I hadn't heard."

"Bit of a shock?"

"Look here," he said. "I badly want a drink, but I haven't any *cash* – except five pounds sterling. I'd be very happy if you would *stand* me one."

It was my turn to say "Of course". I thought for a moment and told the driver the name of a small bar in the Kärntnerstrasse. I didn't think he would want

---

lift, free ride, ride given to a traveller on foot.
hesitate, wait because not sure what to do or say.
cash, ready money, coins and banknotes.
stand, pay for.

jeep

to be seen for a while in a busy British bar full of officers and their wives. This bar seldom had more than one couple in it at a time. The trouble was too that it really only had one drink – a sweet chocolate liqueur – but it seemed to me that Martins did not mind any drink so long as it made him forget. We had a whole room to ourselves; the only couple were next door, and the *waiter*, who knew me, left us alone.

Martins said over his second drink, "I'm sorry, but he was the best friend I ever had."

I said, "Tell me about yourself – and Lime."

"Look here," he said. "I badly need another drink, but I can't keep on asking a stranger. Could you change me a pound into Austrian money?"

"Don't *bother* about that," I said and called the waiter. "You can *treat* me when I come to London. You were going to tell me how you met Lime?"

He looked at his glass, and turned it this way and that. He said, "It was a long time ago. I don't suppose anyone knows Harry the way I do," and I thought of all the things my office knew about him.

"How long?"

"Twenty years – or a bit more. I met him my first *term* at school. I can see the place. I can hear the bell ringing. He was a year older and knew everything about the school. He taught me a lot of things."

waiter

bother, take trouble, be worried.
treat, give food, drink, and so on.
term, part of a school year, for instance 3 months.

He took a quick mouthful of his drink and then turned the glass again as if to see more clearly what there was to see. He said, "It's funny. I can't remember meeting any woman quite as well."

"Was he clever at school?"

"Not the way they wanted him to be. But what things he did think up! I was far better at things like history and English than Harry, but I was hopeless when it came to carrying out his plans." He laughed: he was already beginning, with the help of drink and talk, to throw off the shock of the death. He said, "I was always the one who got caught."

"That was nice for Lime."

"What do you mean?" he asked.

"Well, wasn't it?"

"That was my fault, not his. He could have found someone cleverer if he had wanted to." Certainly, I thought.

"When did you see him last?"

"Oh, he was over in London six months ago for a *medical congress*. You know he was a doctor, though he never *practised*. That was just like him. He just wanted to see if he could do a thing, and then he lost interest. But he used to say it often *came in handy*". And that too was true. It was strange how like the Lime he knew was, to the Lime I knew; it was only that he looked at him in a different light.

---

medical congress, meeting of doctors who come together from many places to learn from each other.
practise, work as a doctor.
came in handy, was of use to him.

Martins said, "One of the things I liked about Harry was his humour." He gave a *grin* which made him look five years younger.

He *whistled* a *tune* – I thought I knew it. "I always remember that. I saw Harry write it. Just in a few minutes on the back of an *envelope*. That was what he always whistled when he had something on his mind." He whistled the tune again, and I knew then who had written it – of course it wasn't Harry. I nearly told him so, but why should I? He looked into his glass, drank what was left, and said, "It's a shame to think of him dying like that."

"It was the best thing that ever happened to him," I said.

He did not understand at once. "The best thing?"

"Yes."

"You mean there wasn't any pain?"

"He was lucky in that way, too."

It was my tone of voice, and not my words that caught Martins' attention. He asked – I could see his right hand tighten – "What do you mean?"

I moved my chair away from him, and said, "I mean, we know all about him at police *headquarters*. He would have gone to prison for a long time – if this had not happened."

"What for?"

---

grin, broad smile.

whistle, produce a sharp sound or series of sounds, as birds do.

tune, melody.

headquarters, place from where orders are sent out; central office.

envelope

"He was the worst *racketeer* who ever came to this city."

I could see him measure the distance between us and decide that he could not reach me from where he sat.

"You're a policeman?" he said.

"Yes."

"I have always hated policemen. They are always stupid."

"Is that the kind of books you write?"

I could see him moving his chair to block my way out. I caught the waiter's eye and he knew what I meant.

Martins said with a smile, "I have to call them sheriffs."

"Been in America?"

"No. Why do you ask?"

"Just interest."

"Because if Harry was a racketeer, I must be one too. We always worked together."

"I am sure he meant you to help. I wouldn't be surprised if he had meant to *give you the baby to hold*. That was his method at school – you told me, didn't you?"

"You are a real policeman, aren't you? So like you to put the blame on a dead man."

He was between me and the door now. "Why

---

racketeer, person making money in a bad and dishonest way.
give you the baby to hold, run away and leave you to take the blame.

don't you policemen catch a few murderers for a change?"

"Well, you could say that murder was part of his *racket.*"

He pushed the table over with one hand and struck at me with the other. Before he could try again my driver had his arms round him. "Be quiet, can't you, sir?" he said.

"Listen, Callaghan, or whatever your name is . . ."

"Calloway, I'm English, not Irish."

"I'm going to make you look the biggest fool in Vienna. There is one dead man you aren't going to *pin* your crimes on."

"I see. You're going to find me the real criminal? It sounds like one of your stories."

"You can let me go, Callaghan. I'd rather let you look the fool you are than give you a black eye. But when I've finished with you, you'll leave Vienna."

I took a couple of pounds' worth of "*bafs*" and stuck them in his pocket.

"These will *see you through* tonight," I said. "And I'll make sure they keep a seat for you on tomorrow's London plane."

"You can't turn me out. My papers are in order."

"Yes, but you need money here, and you can't change your pounds. Let him go."

"Thanks for the drinks."

---

racket, way of getting money which is not honest.
pin, fix.
bafs, banknotes.
see you through, help you through.

2*

"That's all right. I might come and see you off tomorrow."

"I shouldn't waste your time. I won't be there."

"Paine here will show you the way to Sacher's. You can get a bed and dinner there. I'll see to that."

He stepped to one side and struck at me, and I fell against the table. Before he could try again Paine *landed him one* on the nose. I said, "I thought you had promised not to fight."

He *wiped* some blood *away* from his face and said, "Oh, no, I said I would rather make you a fool. I didn't say that I wouldn't give you a black eye."

I had had a long day and was tired of Rollo Martins. When I left the bar, I heard Paine say to the man he had just knocked down, "This way, sir. It's only just round the corner."

---

landed him one, hit him.
wipe away, take away.

Questions

1. How much money could a British subject take with him if he wanted to travel?
2. How could Rollo Martins enter Austria?
3. What happened at Frankfurt?
4. Who is Mr Dexter?
5. Who is J. G. Carey?
6. Who came to meet Martins at the airport in Vienna?
7. What was the name of his hotel?
8. What did Martins know before he got to the second floor?
9. Why was there a black bow over the door handle?
10. Who told him Lime was dead?
11. How had Lime died?
12. Where was the cemetery? What is a cemetery?
13. What is a zone?
14. What is a short cut?
15. Who did Martins go and speak to in the cemetery?

16. Why did the teller of the story follow Martins?
17. What is the name of the teller of the story?
18. Where did the two men go?
19. Where had Martins first met Lime?
20. What do the two men think of Lime?
21. Who did Martins believe had written the tune? Had he?
22. Why did Calloway not like Lime?
23. What did Martins do when Calloway told him what the police thought of Lime?
24. What is Sacher's?

3

What happened next I didn't hear from Paine but from Martins a long time afterwards, and it did prove me to be a fool.

Paine took him to the *porter's desk* and explained there, "This gentleman came in on the plane from London. *Colonel* Calloway says he's to have a room, sir," and left.

"Had you already got a reservation, sir?" the porter asked.

"No. No, I don't think so," Martins said.

"I thought perhaps you might be Mr Dexter. We had a room reserved for a week for Mr Dexter."

Martins said, "Oh, I am Mr Dexter." He told me later that *it occurred to him* that Lime might have

---

colonel, officer ranking below general.
it occurred to him, it came to his mind.

got him a room in that name. A voice said at his elbow, "I'm so sorry you were not met at the plane, Mr Dexter. My name's Crabbin. You got my note?"

Martins held his handkerchief to his mouth and said, "Yes. Yes."

"May I say at once, Mr Dexter, how happy I am to meet you?"

"Good of you."

"Ever since I was a boy, I have thought you the greatest novelist of our time."

Martins looked angrily at Mr Crabbin.

"You have a big Austrian *public*, Mr Dexter."

Martins was thinking hard. "Did you say – room for a week?"

"Yes."

"Very kind of you."

"Mr Schmidt here will give you *tickets* every day, for your meals. But I think you will need some pocket money. We'll fix that. Tomorrow we thought you would like a quiet day to look around."

"Yes."

"Then the day after tomorrow in the evening there is a discussion – on the modern novel. We thought you would like to say a few words."

At that moment Martins was prepared to do anything to get rid of Mr Crabbin and also to get a week's free *board and lodging*. He said, "Of course, of course," into his handkerchief.

---

public, number of people who read his books.
ticket, piece of paper that gives the owner certain rights.
board and lodging, food and a room.

"Excuse me, Mr Dexter, have you got a toothache? I know a very good *dentist.*"

"No. Somebody hit me, that's all."

"Good God. Were they trying to *rob* you?"

"No, it was a soldier. I was trying to give Colonel Callaghan a black eye."

"Never heard of him."

"Heard of Harry Lime?"

"Yes," said Crabbin, "but I didn't really know him."

"I did. He was my best friend."

"A friend of his – an *actress,* you know – is learning English at the Institute. He called once or twice to fetch her."

"Young or old?"

"Oh, young, very young. Not a good actress in my opinion."

---

dentist, doctor taking care of people's teeth.
rob, steal from.
actress, person who acts on the *stage* or in films.

an actress on the stage

Martins remembered the girl by the grave with her hands over her face. He said, "I'd like to meet any friend of Harry's."

"She'll come to hear you speak, I think."

"Austrian?"

"She says she is, but I think she is Hungarian. I should not be surprised if Lime helped her with her papers. She calls herself Schmidt. Anna Schmidt. You can't imagine a young English actress calling herself Smith, can you? And a pretty one, too."

Martins felt he had got all he could from Crabbin, so he said he was tired after a long day, promised to ring up in the morning, accepted ten pounds' worth of "bafs", and went to his room. It seemed to him that he was making money quickly – twelve pounds in less than an hour.

He was tired; he realized that when he lay down on his bed in his boots. Within a minute he was fast asleep. He woke suddenly to hear the telephone ringing by his bed.

A voice said, "Is that Mr Rollo Martins?"

"Yes." It was a change to be himself and not Dexter.

"You wouldn't know me," the voice said, "but I was a friend of Harry Lime."

It was a change too to hear anyone say that he was a friend of Harry Lime. He said, "I'd be glad to meet you."

"I'm just round the corner at the Old Vienna."

"Wouldn't you make it tomorrow? I've had a pretty awful day with one thing and another."

"Harry asked me to see that you were all right. I was with him when he died."

"I thought –" Rollo Martins said and then stopped. He had been going to say, "I thought he died immediately," but he thought better of it. He said instead, "You haven't told me your name."

"Kurtz," the voice said. "I'd offer to come round to you, only, you know, Austrians are not allowed in Sacher's."

"Perhaps we could meet at the Old Vienna in the morning."

"Certainly," the voice said, "if you are quite sure that you are all right till then?"

"How do you mean?"

"Harry had it on his mind that you'd have no money."

Rollo Martins lay back on his bed with the *receiver* to his ear and thought, "Come to Vienna to

receiver

make money." This was the third stranger to offer him money in less than five hours. He said, "I can carry on till I see you."

"Shall we say eleven, then, at the Old Vienna in the Kärntnerstrasse? I'll be in a brown suit and I'll carry one of your books."

"That's fine. How did you get hold of one?"

"Harry gave it to me."

When Martins had said good-night and rung off, he could not help wondering how it was that, if Harry had been able to think of so many things before he died, he had not had a telegram sent to stop him. Hadn't Callaghan said that Lime had died immediately – or without pain, was it? – or had he himself put the words into Callaghan's mouth? It was then that the idea first came to Martins' mind that there was something wrong about Lime's death, something the police had been too stupid to discover. He tried to discover it himself with the help of two cigarettes, but he fell asleep without his dinner and with the mystery still not solved. It had been a long day, but not quite long enough for that.

Questions

1. Where did Paine take Martins?
2. Who had booked a room for him?
3. Why was he to have tickets for his meals?
4. Who had Lime called for at the Institute?
5. What woke up Martins?
6. What did the stranger say about Harry's death?
7. Where was Martins to meet Kurtz the next day?
8. How was he to know Kurtz?
9. What did Martins wonder at?

4

"What I didn't like about him," Martins told me, "was his *toupee*. It was flat and yellow, with the hair cut straight at the back and not fitting close. There must be something *phoney* about a man who wears a toupee."

We were sitting in the Old Vienna at the table he had occupied that first morning with Kurtz, and when he made that remark about the toupee I saw his eyes suddenly catch something. It was a girl – just like any other girl, I thought, going by in the snow outside.

"Something pretty?"

"No. You know, Calloway, a time comes in a man's life when he gives up all that sort of thing . . ."

"I see. I thought you were looking at a girl."

"I was. But only because she reminded me for a moment of Anna – Anna Schmidt."

"Who is she? Isn't she a girl?"

"Oh, yes, in a way."

"What do you mean, in a way?"

"She was Harry's girl."

toupee

---

phoney, false.

"You were telling me about Kurtz," I said.

It appeared that Kurtz was sitting there, making a great show of reading THE LONE RIDER OF SANTA FE. When Martins sat down at his table he said, "It's wonderful how you keep the *tension.*"

"Tension?"

"Yes. At the end of each chapter one is left to guess. . . ."

"So you were a friend of Harry's" Martins said.

"I think his best," but Kurtz added after a short pause, "except you, of course."

"Tell me how he died."

"I was with him. We came out together from the door of his flat and Harry saw a friend he knew across the road – an American called Cooler. He waved to Cooler and started across the road to him when a jeep came tearing round the corner and bowled him over. It was Harry's fault – not the driver's."

"Somebody told me he died immediately."

"I wish he had. He died before the ambulance could reach us, though."

"He could speak, then?"

"Yes."

"What did he say?"

"I can't remember the exact words, Rollo – I may call you Rollo, mayn't I? He always called you that to us. – He was anxious that I should look after you when you arrived. Get your return ticket for you."

---

tension, state of being uncertain and anxious.

"But why didn't you send a telegram to stop me?"

"We did, but it must have missed you."

"There was an *inquest?*"

"Of course."

"Did you know that the police have an idea that Harry was mixed up in some racket?"

"No. But everyone in Vienna is. We sell cigarettes and exchange schillings for bafs and that kind of thing."

"The police meant something worse than that."

inquest, a meeting held by a doctor and some men to find the cause of a death.

"They get funny ideas sometimes."

"I'm going to stay here till I prove them wrong."

Kurtz turned his head sharply. He said, "I don't see what you can do."

"I'm going to start working back from his death. You were there and this man Cooler and the chauffeur. You can give me their addresses."

"I don't know the chauffeur's."

"I can get it from the police. And then there's Harry's girl . . ."

Kurtz said, "It will be hard on her."

"I don't care about her, only about Harry."

"Do you know what it is the police *suspect?*"

"No."

"Do you know," said Kurtz, "you might find something – well, something unpleasant, and that it will take time – and money."

"I've got time and you were going to lend me some money, weren't you?"

"I'm not a rich man," Kurtz said. "I promised Harry to see you were all right and that you got your plane back . . ."

"You needn't worry about the money. But I'll make a *bet* with you that there's something *queer* about Harry's death."

It was a shot in the dark, but already his instinct told him that something was wrong.

---

suspect, think that something is wrong.
bet, promise of money to another person if he is right and you are wrong about something.
queer, strange.

Kurtz had a cup of coffee half-way to his lips and Martins watched him. Then he put down the cup and said, "How do you mean – queer?"

Kurtz had drunk his coffee as if nothing had been said. "Well," he continued, "I don't believe there's anything to find. But just ask me for any help you want."

"I want Cooler's address."

"Certainly. I'll write it down for you. Here it is. In the American zone."

"And yours?"

"I've already put it there. I am in the Russian zone. But I still think you are not very wise."

He picked up THE LONE RIDER. "I'm so proud to have met you. A master of tension," and with one hand on the toupee, and the other passing over his mouth, he brushed a smile from his face as though it had never been.

Questions

1. Who was Martins talking to?
2. Why did Martins look out of the window?
3. How had Harry died?
4. Had he died immediately?
5. What is an inquest?
6. Whose addresses did Martins want?
7. How did Martins know that there was something wrong about Harry's death?
8. Why does Kurtz call Martins a master of tension?

5

card

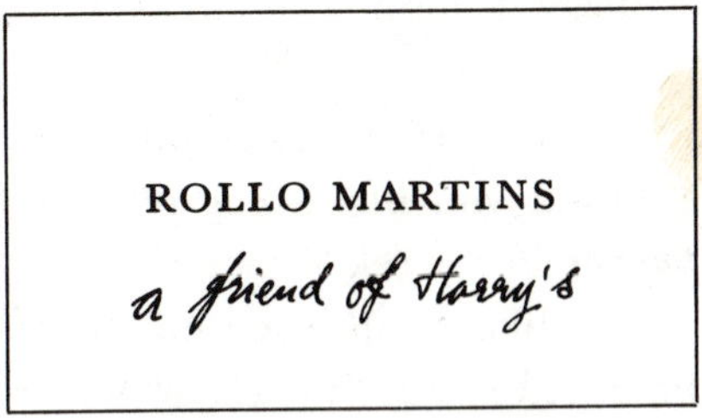

Martins sat on a hard chair just inside the *stage* door of the Josefstadt Theatre. He had sent up his *card* to Anna Schmidt, marking it "a friend of Harry's."

It was cold, even to a man in a heavy overcoat, so that Martins rose and walked up and down under the little windows.

He had had time to think: he was calm now. When a light went out in one of the windows and an actress came down, he didn't even turn to take a look. He thought: Kurtz is right, they are all right, they are all right, I am a fool. I'll just have a word with Anna Schmidt, and then I'll pack and go. He had quite forgotten, he told me, Mr Crabbin.

A voice over his head called "Mr Martins" and he looked up at the face a few feet above his head. It wasn't a beautiful face, just an honest face; dark hair and eyes which in that light looked brown, a large mouth which didn't try to charm. She said, "Will you come up, please? The second door on the right."

There are some people, he explained to me, whom you know at once to be friends. "That was Anna," he said.

---

stage, see picture on page 25.

There was a *kettle* on the gas ring. She said, "Would you like a cup of tea? Someone sent me a *packet* last week."

"I'd like a cup," he said, but if there was one thing he hated it was tea. He watched her while she made it – made it, of course, all wrong: the water was not hot, too few leaves. She said, "I never quite understand why English people like tea."

He drank it quickly like medicine. He said, "I wanted very much to see you. About Harry."

This was the terrible moment; he could see her mouth move.

"Yes?"

"I had known him for twenty years. I was his friend. We were at school together, you know, and after that – there weren't many months running when we didn't meet ..."

She said, "When I got your card, I couldn't say no. But there's nothing really for us to talk about, is there? – Nothing."

"I wanted to hear –"

"He's dead. That's the end. Everything's over, finished. What's the good of talking?"

"We both loved him."

kettle

packet

"I don't know. You can't know a thing like that – afterwards. I don't know anything any more except –"

"Except?"

"That I want to be dead too."

Martins told me, "Then I nearly went away. But instead I asked her one question, 'Do you know a man called Cooler?'"

"An American?" she asked. "I think that was the man who brought me some money when Harry died. I didn't want to take it, but he said Harry had been anxious – at the last moment."

"So he didn't die immediately?"

"Oh, no."

Martins said to me, "I began to wonder why I had got that idea into my head, and then I thought it was only the man in the flat who told me so – no one else. I said to her, 'He must have been very clear in his head at the end – because he remembered about me too. That seems to show that there wasn't really any pain.'"

"That's what I tell myself all the time."

"Did you see the doctor?"

"Once. Harry sent me to him. He was Harry's own doctor. He lived nearby, you see."

Martins suddenly seemed to see before him a street, a body on the ground, and a group of birds gathered. But the picture was gone in a moment, and he thought how strange that they were all there, just at that moment, all Harry's friends – Kurtz, the doctor, this man Cooler; only the two people who loved him seemed to have been missing. He said, "And the driver? Did you hear what he said?"

"It wasn't his fault. I've often heard Harry say what a careful driver he was."

"He knew Harry too?" Another bird flew down and joined the others round the silent figure on the sand who lay face down. Now he could tell it was Harry, by the clothes, lying like a boy asleep in the grass on a hot summer day.

Somebody called outside the window, "Fräulein Schmidt."

She said, "They don't like one to stay too long."

Martins said, "The police say they were going to arrest Harry. They thought he was in a racket."

"Everybody is in a racket."

"I don't believe he was in anything serious."

"No."

"Do you know a man called Kurtz?"

"I don't think so."

"He wears a toupee."

"Oh."

He could tell that that went home. He said, "Don't you think that it was strange they were all there – at the death? Everybody knew Harry. Even the driver, the doctor . . ."

"Fräulein Schmidt," the voice called again.

"I must go."

"I'll walk with you a bit of the way."

They left the theatre. Anna said, "It's better to give up and forget."

"Will you give me the doctor's address?"

They stood still while she wrote it down for him.

"And yours too?"

"Why do you want that?"

"I might have news for you."

"There isn't any news that would do any good now."

Questions

1. Why did Martins walk up and down?
2. What did he know about Anna at once?
3. Why did he not like Anna's tea?
4. Why was there not much for them to talk about?
5. What did she tell him about Harry's death? How did she know?
6. What did she tell him about the driver?
7. Whose address did she give him?
8. What were Anna's feelings when told of Harry's death?

6

An amateur detective has the advantage over the *professional* that he does not work set hours. Rollo Martins did as much work in one day as one of my men would have done in two. And he had this advantage, too, that he was Harry's friend.

Dr Winkler was at home. Perhaps he would not have been at home to a police officer. Again Martins had written on his card: A friend of Harry Lime's.

Dr Winkler's waiting-room reminded Martins of an *antique shop*. There were more *crucifixes* than he could count, and most of them as old as the seventeenth century. There were *statues* in wood and *ivory*. There were little bits of bone marked with the names of *saints* and set in *oval frames*. What a strange thing for Saint Susanna's fingerbone to come to rest in Dr Winkler's waiting-room. He heard a *sneeze* behind him.

Dr Winkler was the cleanest doctor Martins had ever seen. He was very small and neat, in a black tail-coat and a high stiff collar. He sneezed again; perhaps he was cold because he was so clean. He said, "Mr Martins?"

---

professional, person who makes a business of something that others do for pleasure.
antique shop, shop selling very old furniture.
ivory, the big teeth of elephants are made of ivory.
saint, very holy person.
sneeze, blow air through one's nose when one has a cold.

Martins answered, "Dr Winkler?"
"Dr Winkler."
"You've got a number of interesting things here."
"Yes."
"These saints' bones . . ."

"The bones of *chickens* and rabbits." Dr Winkler took a large white handkerchief and blew his nose carefully twice. You expected him to throw away the handkerchief after one use. "Would you mind, Mr Martins, telling me what I can do for you? I have a patient waiting."

"We were both friends of Harry Lime."

"I was his doctor."

"I arrived too late for the inquest. Harry had invited me out here to help him in something. I don't quite know what. I didn't hear of his death till I arrived."

"Very sad," said Dr Winkler.

"Of course I want to hear all I can."

"There is nothing I can tell you that you don't know. He was knocked over by a car. He was dead when I arrived."

"You are quite certain that it was an *accident?*"

Dr Winkler put out a hand and touched a crucifix. "I was not there. I only know what he died of."

Martins said, "The police thought he was in a racket. It seemed to me that he might have been murdered – or even killed himself."

"I could not say," Dr Winkler said.

"Do you know a man called Cooler?"

"I don't think so."

chicken

---

accident, something bad that happens, for instance a person being killed by falling from a great height.

"He was there when Harry was killed."

"Then of course I have met him. He wears a toupee."

"That was Kurtz."

Dr Winkler was not only the cleanest doctor Martins had ever met; you also had a feeling that you could not for a moment doubt that what he said was true. He said, "There was a second man there."

"Had you been Harry's doctor for long?"

"For about a year."

"Well it's good of you to have seen me." Dr Winkler bowed. "I mustn't keep you from your patients any longer." He turned away from the doctor. "That's a strange crucifix," he said. "Why are the arms above the head?"

"It is *Jansenist,* and in their view He died only for the few."

Questions

1. What was Dr Winkler's waiting-room like?
2. Why did Dr Winkler blow his nose?
3. What did Dr Winkler know about Lime's death?

Jansenist, belonging to a party in the Roman Catholic Church holding that the natural human will is unable to do good.

7

As I see it, it would still have been possible, at this moment, for Rollo Martins to have left Vienna safely. Nobody had given anything away. When Rollo Martins left Dr Winkler's he was in no danger. He could have gone to bed at Sacher's and slept with a quiet mind. Unfortunately for him he chose to go back to Harry's flat. He wanted to talk to the little man who had said he had seen the accident – or had he really not said so much?

Perhaps the little man – who bore the name of Koch – had drunk a glass too much, perhaps he had simply spent a good day at the office, but this time, when Rollo Martins rang his bell, he was friendly and quite ready to talk. "Ah, I remember you. You are Herr Lime's friend."

He led the way into the sitting-room. "Ah, in the old days I would have offered you a cup of coffee, but now –"

Martins offered him a cigarette. He said, "Did you tell me that you had seen the accident?"

Herr Koch looked at his wife. "The inquest is over. There is no harm. The gentleman is a friend. Yes, I saw the accident, but you are the only one who knows. When I say that I saw it, perhaps I should say that I heard it. But I got to the window in time to see them carry the body to the house."

"Was he in great pain?"

"He was dead."

"But the others say that he did not die at once."

"Perhaps they do not know death as well as I do."

"He was dead, of course, when the doctor arrived. He told me that."

"He was dead at once. You can take my word for it."

"I think, Herr Koch, that you should have given *evidence* at the inquest."

"One must look after oneself, Herr Martins. I was not the only one who should have been there."

"What do you mean?"

"There were three people who helped to carry your friend to the house."

"I know – two men and the driver."

"The driver stayed where he was. He was very much shaken, poor man."

"Three men . . . Can you describe them?"

But Herr Koch could not describe them. He had noticed only the man with the toupee. He had seen them from above. They had not looked up, and he had quickly looked away and closed the window. Martins no longer doubted that murder had been done. Why else had they *lied* about the moment of death? And the third man? Who was he?

He said, "Did you see Herr Lime go out?"

"No."

It struck Martins that there was nothing – except

---

evidence, what you say you have seen which can clear up things.

lied, not told the truth.

the word of Kurtz and Cooler and the driver – to prove that in fact Harry had been killed at that moment.

"Herr Martins, it just occurs to me – you are staying in Vienna?"

"Yes."

"If you want a place to live, you might get Herr Lime's flat."

"Who has the keys?"

"I have them."

"Could I see the flat?"

Herr Koch led the way into the flat that had been Harry's. In the little dark hall there was still the smell of cigarette smoke – the Turkish cigarettes that Harry always smoked. In the sitting-room the chairs had been pushed up against the walls. In the bedroom the bed had been neatly made with clean *sheets*. "You see," Herr Koch said, "it is quite ready for a newcomer. My wife has cleaned up."

"Were there no papers, Herr Koch?"

"Herr Lime was always a very *tidy* man. His *briefcase* was full, but his friend took that away."

"His friend?"

"Yes, the gentleman with the toupee."

briefcase

---

sheet, large piece of linen used to sleep on or under.
tidy, neat and with things in order.

It was possible, of course, that Lime had not died so *unexpectedly,* and that he might have hoped that Martins would arrive in time to help. He said to Herr Koch, "I believe my friend was murdered."

"Murdered?" said Herr Koch. "I would not have asked you in here if I had thought you would talk such nonsense."

"Why should it be nonsense?"

"We do not have murders in this zone. And you must leave at once, please." He took Martins through the hall, and *slammed* the door after him.

Later, when I was questioning Martins, I said to him, "Did you see anybody at all on the stairs, or in the street outside?"

"Nobody." And I believed him. He said, "I noticed myself how quiet and dead the whole street looked. It was so very silent. I could hear my own feet *creaking* in the snow."

"Of course it proves nothing. Somebody could easily follow you and hide in a doorway."

"Yes."

"Or your whole story may be phoney."

"Yes."

"You came out here to join Lime, perhaps to help him . . ."

Martins said to me, "What was this racket you keep talking about?"

---

unexpectedly, suddenly, without warning.
slam, shut with a noise.
creak, make the sound of a door which is not oiled, or of feet on snow.

"I would have told you when I first saw you, but now I don't think it will be wise to do so. I don't like the people you meet, and besides information is not complete."

"I bet it isn't. I could *invent* a better detective than you in my bath."

On returning to Sacher's hotel after his *interview* with Herr Koch he had a note from Crabbin waiting for him. "I have been trying to find you all day," Crabbin wrote. "We must get together today and work out a programme for you. This morning by telephone I have arranged for you to go to Innsbruck and Salzburg to give *lectures*. But we must agree on what you are going to speak about. There are a great many people here who would like to meet you, and I want to arrange a party for early next week. But for all this I must have a word with you. You will be at the meeting tomorrow night, won't you? We all expect you at 8.30, and look forward to your coming. I will send transport to the hotel at 8.15 sharp."

Rollo Martins read the letter and went to bed.

---

invent, think out.
interview, meeting, conversation.
lecture, talk, speech on a planned subject.

Questions

1. How did Herr Koch receive Martins?
2. Why did Herr Koch look at his wife?
3. What did Herr Koch say about Harry's death?
4. How many people had he seen carrying Harry to the house?
5. Why could Herr Koch not describe them?
6. Why did Martins go and see the flat?
7. Why did Herr Koch say that they had no murders in his zone?
8. What did Martins find when he came back to his hotel?

8

It was nearly five o'clock when Rollo Martins reached Cooler's flat, which was over an ice-cream bar in the American zone; the bar was full of *G.I.'s* with their girls, and the noise of long spoons and laughter followed him up the stairs. Again the card marked "Harry's friend" opened the doors for him. Cooler was in officer's uniform. His handshake was the most friendly act that Martins had *encountered* in Vienna.

"Any friend of Harry is all right with me," Cooler said. "I've heard of you, of course."

"From Harry?"

"I'm a great reader of Westerns," Cooler said, and Martins believed him as he had not believed Kurtz.

"I wondered – you were there, weren't you? – if you would tell me about Harry's death."

"It was a terrible thing," Cooler said. "I was just crossing the road to go to Harry. He and Kurtz were on the other side of the street. Maybe if I hadn't started across the road, he would have stayed where he was. But he saw me and stepped off to meet me and this jeep – it was terrible. Have a whisky, Mr Martins. It's silly of me but I get shaken up when I think of it." He said as he put in the soda-water, "In spite of this uniform, I had never seen a man killed before."

G.I., American soldier (Government Issue).
encounter, meet, see, experience.

"Was the other man in the car?"

Cooler took a long drink. "What man would you be speaking about, Mr Martins?"

"I was told there was another man there."

"I don't know how you got that idea." He poured out two more drinks. "There were just the three of us – me and Mr Kurtz and the driver. The doctor, of course. I expect you were thinking of the doctor."

"This man I was talking to happened to look out of the window – he has the flat next to Harry's – and he said he saw three men and the driver. That's before the doctor arrived."

"He didn't say that at the inquest. It was his duty." Cooler looked at his glass. "It is strange, Mr Martins, with accidents. You'll never get two people who agree on what they have seen. Even Kurtz and I did not agree on details. Things happen so quickly, and then you have to try to remember afterwards. I think he was too busy trying to find out what had happened before and what happened after to *distinguish* the four of us."

"The four?"

"I was counting Harry. What else did he see, Mr Martins?"

"Nothing of interest – except he says Harry was dead when he was carried to the house."

"Well, he was dying. Have another drink, Mr Martins?"

"No, I don't think I will."

---

distinguish, see the difference between, tell apart.

"Well, I'd like one. I was very fond of your friend, Mr Martins, and I don't like talking about it."

"Perhaps one more – to keep you company. Do you know Anna Schmidt?"

"Harry's girl? I met her once, that's all. I helped Harry fix her papers. Not a thing one should say to strangers."

"What was wrong?"

"She was Hungarian and her father had been a Nazi, so they said."

"You took her some money from Harry, didn't you?"

"Yes, but I wouldn't have mentioned that. Did she tell you?"

The telephone rang, and Cooler emptied his glass. "Hullo," he said. "Why, yes. This is Colonel Cooler."

Then he sat with the receiver at his ear, while some voice a long way off *drained* into the room. "Yes," he said once. "Yes." He seemed to look a long way behind Martins. He said, "You did quite right," and then, "Of course they will be sent. I gave you my word. Goodbye."

He put the receiver down. It was as if he was trying to remember something he had to do. Martins said, "Had you heard anything of this racket the police talk about?"

"I'm sorry. What's that?"

"They say Harry was mixed up in some racket."

---

drain, flow slowly.

"Oh, no," Cooler said. "No. That's quite impossible. He had a great sense of duty."

"Kurtz seemed to think it was possible."

"Kurtz does not understand how an Englishman feels," Cooler answered.

Questions

1. Where did Cooler live?
2. What did Cooler do when Martins said he thought there was a third man?
3. What did Martins tell Cooler?
4. What did Cooler say that might show that Herr Koch was right?
5. Why did Cooler not really hear what Martins said to him after the telephone call?

9

It was nearly dark when Martins made his way along the banks of the canal. He passed the door of the Military Police station, walked round the corner of the street where Sacher's lay and went on. He moved towards the only girl he knew in Vienna.

I asked him how he knew where she lived. Oh, he said, he'd looked up the address she had given him the night before, in bed, studying a map. He wanted to know his way about, and he was good with maps. He could remember *turnings* and street names easily because he always went one way on foot.

He hadn't, of course, known that she would be in, but she was, if you could call it being in, sitting alone in a cold room, with the bed arranged as a divan. He said, "I thought I'd just look in and look you up. You see, I was passing . . ."

"Passing? Where to?"

"I had too much whisky with Colonel Cooler. I needed a walk and I just happened to find myself this way."

"I can't give you a drink here. Except tea. There's some of that packet left."

"No, no, thank you." He said, "You are busy?"

"I ought to be."

"Can I stay a little?"

"I wish you would." He sat down on the divan,

---

turning, place where one street meets another.

and he told me a long time later that there it was he took his second real look at her.

"One of those bad days?" he asked.

"It's always bad about this time." She explained, "He used to look in, and when I heard you ring, just for a moment I thought . . ." She sat down on a hard chair opposite him and said, "Please talk. You knew him. Just tell me anything."

And so he talked. The sky became dark outside the window while he talked. He noticed after a while that their hands had met. He said to me, "I never meant to fall in love, not with Harry's girl."

"When did it happen?" I asked him.

"It was very cold and I got up to close the window *curtains.* I only noticed my hand was on hers when I took it away. As I stood up I looked down at her face and she was looking up. It wasn't a beautiful face – that was the trouble. It was a face to live with, *day in, day out*. I had always thought it was beauty one loved in a woman. I stood there at the curtains, waiting to pull them, looking out. I couldn't see anything but my own face, looking back into the room, looking for her. She said, 'And what did Harry do that time?' and I wanted to say, 'Don't let us talk about Harry. He's dead. The dead are made to be forgotten.' Instead, of course, all I said was, 'What do you think? He just whistled his old tune as if nothing was the matter,' and I whistled it to her as well as I could. I heard her catch her breath, and I looked round and before I could think I'd already said, 'He's dead. You can't go on remembering him for ever.'"

She said, "I know, but perhaps something will happen first."

"What do you mean – something happen?"

"Oh, I mean, perhaps there will be another war, or I'll die, or . . ."

"You'll forget him in time. You'll fall in love again."

"I know, but I don't want to. Don't you see I don't want to."

So Rollo Martins came back from the window and sat down on the divan again. When he had risen half a minute before he had been the friend of Harry

---

day in, day out, every day.

comforting Harry's girl; now he was a man in love with Anna Schmidt who had been in love with a man they had both once known called Harry Lime. He didn't speak again that evening about the past. Instead he began to tell her of the people he had seen. "I can believe anything of Winkler," he told her, "but Cooler – I liked Cooler. He was the only one of his friends who stood up for Harry. The trouble is, if Cooler is right, then Koch is wrong, and I really thought I had something there."

"Who's Koch?"

He explained how he had returned to Harry's flat and he described his interview with Koch, the story of the third man.

"If it's true," she said, "it's very important. And it means that they lied, Kurtz and Cooler."

"They might have lied to keep a friend out of trouble – if he was a friend."

"Yet another friend – on the spot. And how can Cooler be telling the truth then?"

"What do we do? Koch turned me out of his flat."

"He won't turn me out," she said, "or his wife won't."

They walked up the long road to the flat together; the snow *clogged* on their shoes and made them move slowly. Anna Schmidt said, "Is it far?"

"Not very far now. Do you see that group of people up the road? It's somewhere about there." The group was like a spot of ink on the whiteness. When

---

clogged, stuck to their shoes and made their going difficult.

they came a little nearer Martins said, "I think that's his house. What do you think this is, what are they doing here?"

Anna Schmidt stopped. She said, "Who else have you told about Koch?"

"Only you and Cooler. Why?"

"I am afraid. It reminds me . . ." She was looking at the crowd. "Let's go away," she begged him.

"You're *crazy*. We're on to something here, something big . . ."

"I'll wait for you."

"But you're going to talk to him."

"Find out first what all those people . . ."

He walked slowly on alone. When he reached the crowd, he knew for certain that it was the house. A man looked hard at him and said, "Are you another of them?"

"What do you mean?"

"The police."

"No. What are they doing?"

"They've been in and out all day."

"What's everybody waiting for?"

"They want to see him brought out."

"Who?"

"Herr Koch."

"What's he done?"

"Nobody knows that yet. They can't make up their minds in there – he might have killed himself, or it might be murder."

---

crazy, mad, silly.

"Herr Koch?"

"Of course."

A child cried, "They are coming out."

A group of policemen carried a *stretcher* out. The man said, "They can't get an ambulance into this street because of the ruins. They have to carry it round the corner." Frau Koch came out at the tail of the *procession.* Someone gave her a hand and she looked round at this crowd of strangers.

Walking back down the street towards Anna, he looked back once. He said to Anna, "Koch has been murdered. Come away from here." He walked as fast as the snow would let him. He didn't listen when

---

procession, people walking in a group or a line.

Anna said to him, "Then what Koch said was true. There was a third man,"nor a litte later when she said, "It must have been murder. You don't kill a man to hide anything less."

Martins said, "You had better go home alone. I'll keep away from you a little while till things are clearer."

Before she left him, she said, "Be careful. Koch knew so very little and they murdered him. You know as much as Koch."

At Sacher's Mr. Schmidt said, "Colonel Calloway has been in, asking for you, sir. I think you'll find him in the bar."

"Back in a moment," Martins said and walked straight out of the hotel again: he wanted time to think. But immediately he stepped outside a man came forward, touched his cap, and said, "Please, sir." He flung open the door of a car and pressed Martins to get in.

The driver drove too fast on the frozen road, and Martins protested. All he got in reply was a sentence containing the word "orders" – the rest he could not hear. "Have you orders to kill me?" Martins said and got no reply at all.

"Is it far?" But the driver paid no attention at all. At least, Martins thought, I am not under arrest: they have not sent a guard; I am being invited – wasn't that the word they used? – to visit the station.

The car drew up, and the driver led the way up the stairs; he rang the bell of a great double door, and Martins heard many voices behind it. He turned sharply to the driver and said, "Where the hell . . .?" but the driver was already half-way down the stairs, and already the door was opening. He heard but he could hardly see Mr Crabbin. "Oh, Mr Dexter, we have been so anxious, but better late than never. Let me introduce you to . . ."

He said to Mr Crabbin, "I'm sorry but . . ."

"Don't think any more about it," Mr Crabbin said. "One cup of coffee and then let's go on to the discussion. We have a very good gathering tonight." A young man placed a cup in his hand, another put sugar in before he could say that he preferred his coffee without. A third young man said into his ear, "Would you mind signing one of your books, Mr Dexter?" A large woman in black came up to him and said, "I don't mind if others hear me, but I don't like your books. I think a novel should tell a good story."

"So do I," Martins said hopelessly.

An old lady said, "I do not read many English books, Mr Dexter, but I am told that yours . . ."

"Do you mind drinking up?" Crabbin said and led him into an inner room where a number of *elderly* people were sitting on a *semi-circle* of chairs waiting.

Martins was not able to tell me very much about the meeting; he was still thinking of Herr Koch's death. I am sure he gave a very good talk, I have heard him give that talk so often. And then came

---

elderly, not old and not young, becoming old.
semi-circle, half of a circle.

question time. A woman wearing a brown hat said, "May I ask Mr Dexter if he is writing another book?"

"Oh, yes – yes."

"May I ask the title?"

"THE THIRD MAN," Martins said.

"Mr Dexter, could you tell us what writer has *chiefly* influenced you?"

Martins, without thinking, said, "Grey." He meant, of course, the author of 'Riders of the Purple Sage', and he was pleased to find that people liked his answer – except an elderly lady who asked, "Grey. What Grey? I do not know that name."

Martins said, "Zane Grey – I don't know any other," and did not quite understand the laughter that came from the English people present.

"That is a little joke of Mr Dexter's," said Crabbin. "He meant Gray, the poet."

"And he is called Zane Grey?"

"That was Mr Dexter's joke. Zane Grey wrote what we call Westerns – cheap novels about cowboys and bandits."

"He is not a great writer?"

"No, no. Far from it," Mr Crabbin said.

Martins could not have said how he got through the rest of the evening. Perhaps he was helped by some of the people who got into a discussion about the film made from a popular American novel. He remembered very little more before Crabbin was making a speech to thank him. Then one of the

---

chiefly, mainly, mostly.

young men led him to a table filled with books and asked him to sign them.

"What have I got to do?"

"Just put your name in the books. That's all they expect. But I would be so happy if you would just write a little something in my copy."

Martins took his pen and wrote: "From B. Dexter, author of The Lone Rider of Santa Fé," and the young man read it, took the book and went to show it to Mr Crabbin who smiled and moved his head up and down, up and down. "B. Dexter, B. Dexter, B. Dexter," Martins wrote quickly – it was not, after all, a lie. Every time he took another book and looked up, he met Crabbin's eye. People were beginning to leave, when suddenly in the *mirror* Martins saw a military policeman. He seemed to be having a discussion with one of Mr Crabbin's young men. There was only one book left to sign. He wrote "B. Dexter" and made for the door.

"And this gentleman?" the policeman asked.

"It's Mr Benjamin Dexter," the young man said.

"*Lavatory.* Is there a lavatory?" Martins asked.

"I understand a Mr Rollo Martins came here in one of your cars."

"A mistake, a mistake."

"Second door on the left," the young man said.

Martins took his coat as he went and made down the stairs. On the first floor he heard someone coming up and, looking over, saw Paine, whom I had sent to *identify* him. He opened a door and shut it behind him. He could hear Paine go by. The room where he stood was dark, a sound made him turn.

He could see nothing and the sound died away. Outside somebody called, "Mr Dexter, Mr Dexter." Then a new sound started. It was like somebody whispering. Martins said, "Is anybody there?" and the sound stopped again. He could *stand* no more of it. He took out his *lighter.* Footsteps went by and

lighter

switch

knob

---

lavatory, toilet, place where one can wash.
identify, recognize, prove to be a certain person.
stand, bear.

down the stairs. He *scraped* and scraped at the little wheel and no light came. Somebody moved in the dark. He asked once more with the anger of fear, "Is anybody there?" He felt for a *switch*, first to his right hand and then to his left. Then he was afraid that he had lost the door and felt for the *knob*. He was far less afraid of the police than of the darkness, and he had no idea of the noise he was making.

Paine heard it from the bottom of the stairs and came back. He switched on the light, and Martins saw it under the door. He opened the door, and smiling at Paine, turned back to take a look at the room. The eyes of a *parrot* stared back at him. "We were looking for you, sir," said Paine. "Colonel Calloway wants a word with you."

"I lost my way," Martins said.

"Yes, sir. We thought that was what had happened."

parrot

---

scrape, rub with something hard so that a noise is made.

Questions

1. How did Martins find his way?
2. What did Anna think of his coming to see her?
3. What happened while they were talking?
4. Why did he close the window curtains?
5. Why did she not want to forget Harry?
6. Why did they walk back to Koch's flat?
7. What did they see when they came near the house?
8. What had happened in the house?
9. Who carried Herr Koch out?
10. Why was Martins to be careful?
11. What happened when he came back to the hotel?
12. What happened outside the hotel?
13. Where did the driver take him?
14. What did the young man ask him to do?
15. Why could Martins not remember much of what had happened?
16. Why did the English people present laugh?
17. Where did Martins first see the policeman?
18. Why did Martins want to go to the lavatory?
19. What happened in the room?
20. What had frightened him?

10

I had *kept a careful record* of Martins' movements from the moment I knew that he had not caught the plane home. He had been seen with Kurtz, and at the Josefstadt Theatre; I knew about his visit to Dr Winkler and to Colonel Cooler, his first return to the house where Harry had lived. For some reason my man lost him between Cooler's and Anna Schmidt's flats; he reported that Martins had walked around a lot. I tried to pick him up at the hotel and just missed him. It seemed to me that the time had come for another interview .

I put a good wide table between us and gave him a cigarette. I asked him about Kurtz and he told me what I knew already. I then asked him about Anna Schmidt and I gathered from his reply that he must have been with her after visiting Colonel Cooler; that filled in one of the missing points. "You've been getting around," I said, "quite a bit. And have you found out anything about your friend?"

"Oh, yes," he said. "It was under your nose but you didn't see it."

"What?"

"That he was murdered." That took me by surprise. I had at one time thought he might have killed himself but I had given up that idea.

"Go on," I said. He tried not to mention Koch and

---

kept a careful record, carefully gathered information.

talked about somcbody who had seen the accident, so I didn't at first understand why the third man should be so important.

"He didn't *turn up* at the inquest, and the others lied to keep him out."

"It was an accident, and why get another man in trouble?"

"There was more to it than that. The little man who told me about it – they've murdered him. You see, they didn't know what else he had seen."

"Now we have it," I said. "You mean Koch."

"Yes."

"As far as we know, you were the last person to see him alive. The Austrian police think you might have killed him. Who else knew about your visit?"

"I told Cooler." He said, "Suppose after I left he telephoned the story to someone – to the third man. They had to stop Koch's mouth."

"Koch was killed soon after nine. You returned to Sacher's at nine-thirty. Where were you before that?"

"Walking around and trying to think things over."

"You can't prove that this is true?"

"No."

I wanted to frighten him, so it was no use telling him that he had been followed all the time.

"Can I have a cigarette?"

"Yes."

He said, "How did you know I went to Koch's? That was why you wanted me here, wasn't it?"

---

turn up, appear.

"The Austrian police . . ."

"They hadn't identified me."

"Colonel Cooler telephoned me."

"Then that lets him out. If he had been in it, he wouldn't have wanted to tell you my story – Koch's story, I mean."

"To tell you the truth, Cooler irritates me. Of course he doesn't know that I know about his racket."

"Is he in a racket, too?"

"I should think he has made a good deal of money selling *tyres*. But let the Americans look after their own people."

"Is that the kind of thing Harry was up to?"

"No. It was of a more serious kind."

He said, "You know this business – Koch's death – has shaken me. Perhaps Harry did get mixed up in something pretty bad. Perhaps he was trying to clear out again, and that was why they murdered him."

"Or perhaps," I said, "they wanted a bigger *share* of the money."

He did not get angry this time. He said, "I'm sorry about the other day."

"That's all right," I said, "I'll show you enough of the facts in Lime's case for you to understand. But I tell you, it's going to be a shock."

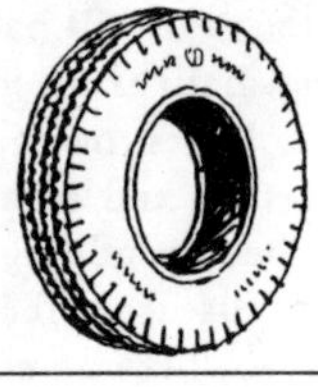

tyre

share, part.

It couldn't help being a shock. The war and the peace let loose a great number of rackets, but none worse than the *penicillin* racket. Penicillin in Austria was *supplied* only to military hospitals. No *civilian* hospital could get it. To begin with the penicillin racket was not too bad; the stuff was stolen in military hospitals and sold to Austrian doctors for very high sums. But then the racket began to get *organised;* the big men saw big money in it. They began to *dilute* the penicillin with coloured water. Martins did not see the point. He said, "I suppose that makes the stuff useless."

I said, "We wouldn't worry so much if that was all, but just think. At the best you can say that the use of this stuff takes away the effect of penicillin in the future – well, it's pretty bad. But men have lost their arms and legs this way – and their lives. But what shocked me most was visiting the children's hospital here. They had bought some of this stuff for use against *meningitis.* A number of children died, and a number *went off their heads.*"

"You haven't proved yet that Harry –"

"We are coming to that now," I said. "Just sit still and listen. We put one of our men as an *orderly*

---

penicillin, stuff that can kill bacteria.
supply, hand over, deliver after selling.
civilian, not for soldiers, not military.
organise, get together and arrange.
dilute, make thinner by adding water.
meningitis, serious disease affecting the brain and the nerves.
went off their heads, became mad.
orderly, soldier who carries out the orders of an officer.

in the British Military Hospital, and at last he found the man who stole the penicillin – a man called Harbin. But even this led us only as far as Kurtz."

"Kurtz," said Martins. "But why haven't you arrested him?"

"We are going to," I said.

"Kurtz was a big step forward, for with Kurtz Lime sometimes put things on paper. Look at this." And I showed Martins a short note written by Lime.

"It's Harry's hand." He read it through. "I don't see anything wrong."

"No, but now read this note from Harbin to Kurtz – which we dictated. Look at the date. This note is the result."

He read them both through twice.

"You see what I mean?"

He didn't say a word. Who would when he sees a world laid in ruins before him, and this was the ruin of all his happy memories, the dreams, the walks, a world of easy friendship. While he sat there, looking at his hands and saying nothing, I fetched a bottle of whisky and poured out two big glasses. "Drink that," I said, and he did.

"Are you certain that he was the real *boss?*"

"We've not found anyone behind him so far."

"Suppose someone had forced him into it, as you forced Harbin."

"It's possible."

---

boss, chief.

"And they murdered him in case he talked when he was arrested."

"It's not impossible."

"I'm glad they did," he said. "And in that case I might as well be getting back to England."

"I'd rather you didn't just now. The Austrian police might want a word with you."

"I see," he said.

"When we've found the third man . . ." I said.

"I'd like to hear him *squeal*," he said.

Questions

1. Why did Calloway get a wide table between them?
2. What had Colonel Cooler done after Martins had spoken to him?
3. What was the racket Harry Lime was in?
4. Where did the racketeers get the penicillin?
5. What did they do with it?
6. Why did Martins look at his hands?
7. How did Calloway prove that Lime was a racketeer?
8. Why couldn't Martins go back to England now?

---

squeal, make a loud, high sound because one is in pain.

11

After he left me, Martins went straight off to *drink himself silly.* He chose a night club to do it in, and had drink after drink. He moved on to Maxim's and a place called Chez Victor where the *heating* had failed and people sat in overcoats drinking cocktails. It must have been about three in the morning when he climbed the stairs to Anna's room. He was now nearly *sober* and had only one idea in his head, that she must know about Harry too.

He said, "Anna, I've found out everything."

"Come in," she said. "You don't want to wake the whole house." She was in a *dressing-gown;* the divan

---

drink himself silly, drink so much that he would forget everything.
heating, the system of making a house warm.
sober, not drunk.

had become a bed, the kind of bed that showed how sleepless the person in it had been.

"Now," she said, "what is it? I thought you were going to keep away. Are the police after you?"

"No."

"You didn't really kill that man, did you?"

"Of course not."

"You're drunk, aren't you?"

"I am a bit," he said. "I'm sorry."

"Why? I would like a drink myself."

He said, "I've been with the British police. They know I didn't do it. But I've learnt everything from them. Harry was in a racket – a bad racket. He was no good at all. We were both wrong."

"You'd better tell me," Anna said. She sat down on the bed and he told her, in a rather *confused* way. I imagine, about the penicillin and the dead children. He stopped and they were silent.

She said, "Is that all?"

"Yes."

"You were sober when they told you? They really proved it?"

"Yes. So that, you see, was Harry."

"I'm glad he is dead now," she said. "I wouldn't have wanted him to be in prison."

"But can you understand how Harry – your Harry – my Harry – could have got mixed up? I feel as though he had never really existed, that we'd dreamed

---

confused, not putting things together in the right way, mixed up.

him. Was he laughing at fools like us all the time?"

"He may have been. What does it matter?" she said. "Sit down. Don't worry. If he was alive now, he might be able to explain, but we've got to remember him as he was to us."

"Those children –"

She said angrily, "Harry was real. He was Harry. He was in a racket. He did bad things. What about it? He was the man we knew."

He said, "Don't talk such nonsense. Don't you see that I love you?"

She looked at him in surprise. "You?"

"Yes, me."

She said, "But I don't even know what colour your eyes are."

"Can't you get him out of your mind?"

"No."

He said, "As soon as they have cleared up this Koch murder, I'm leaving Vienna. I can't feel interested any longer in whether Kurtz killed Harry – or the third man. But you still love him. You love a bandit, a murderer."

"I loved a man," she said. "I told you – a man is still a man even if you find out more about him."

"I hate the way you talk."

"I didn't ask you to come."

"You make me angry."

She laughed. "You are so comic. You come here at three in the morning – a stranger – and say you love me. Then you get angry. What do you expect me to do – or say?"

"I haven't seen you laugh before. Do it again. I like it."

"Come away from the window. There are no curtains."

"There's nobody to see." But he wasn't quite sure: a long shadow that had moved stood still again. He said, "You still love Harry, don't you?"

"Yes."

"Perhaps I do. I don't know." He said, "I'll be going."

He walked quickly away. He didn't turn round to see if he was followed. But passing by the end of the street, he happened to see, just around the corner, pressed against a wall, a thick figure. Martins stopped and stared. It looked like somebody he knew. Perhaps it was one of those who had followed him to see where he was going. Martins stood there, staring at the silent figure who stared back at him. A policeman, perhaps, or one of those men who had forced Harry into the racket and then killed him – or even possibly the third man?

He called sharply, "Do you want anything?" and there was no reply. He called again, "Answer, can't you?" and an answer came, for a window curtain was drawn back by some sleeper he had awakened, and the light fell across the street and lit up the face of Harry Lime.

the »kiosk«

Questions

1. At what time of the night did Martins go to see Anna?
2. What did Anna say when Martins said that he loved her?
3. What did he see through the window?
4. Where did the light come from?
5. Who did he see in the street?

12

"Do you believe in *ghosts?*" Martins said to me.

"Do you?"

"I do now."

"I also believe that drunken men see things – sometimes *rats,* sometimes worse."

He hadn't come to me at once with his story – only the danger to Anna Schmidt drove him back into my office. He said, "If it had been just the face, I wouldn't have worried. I'd been thinking of Harry, and I might easily have mistaken a stranger. The light was turned off again at once, you see, and the man moved away down the street – if he was a man. There was no turning just there, but I was so surprised that I gave him another thirty yards' start. He came to one of those newspaper *kiosks* and for a moment was out of sight. I ran after him. It only took ten seconds to reach the kiosk, but the strange thing was he never appeared again. I reached the kiosk. There wasn't anybody there, and the street was empty."

"What did you do then?"

"I had to have another drink. My nerves were all in pieces."

rat

ghost

"Didn't that bring him back?"

"No, but it sent me back to Anna's."

I don't think he would have come to me with this silly story if it had not been for what happened to Anna. My theory, when he did tell me the story, was that somebody had watched him, and that this somebody had warned a member of the penicillin *ring* by telephone. Things happened fast that night.

When Rollo Martins went drunkenly back at four o'clock to tell Anna that he had seen the ghost of Harry, he was told by a porter who had not yet gone back to sleep that she had been taken away by the *International Patrol.*

What happened was this. Half-way through the patrol, the Russian policeman directed the car to the street where Anna lived. The British policeman that night was new to the job: he didn't realise, till his *colleagues* told him, that they had entered a British zone. He spoke a little German and no French, and the Frenchman gave up trying to explain to him. The American took on the job. "It's all right by me," he said, "but is it all right by you?" The British policeman touched the Russian's shoulder, and the latter turned his face and sent a stream of language at him which he did not understand. Outside the house where Anna lived the American *took a hand in the game* and asked in German what it was all about.

---

ring, group of people working together.
patrol, group of soldiers or policemen.
colleague, fellow-worker.
took a hand in the game, dealt with the matter, interfered.

The Russian dug out a few words of German and waved some papers. As far as they could understand, a Russian woman wanted by the Russian police was living there without papers. They went upstairs and the Russian tried Anna's door. It was locked, but he put his shoulder to it, and it flew open. Anna was in bed, though I don't suppose she was asleep.

There is a lot of comedy in these situations if you are not in them. The Russian, you see, refused to leave the room while Anna dressed, the Englishman refused to remain in the room, the American wouldn't leave a girl alone with a Russian soldier, so he turned his back, and the Frenchman – well, I think the Frenchman must have thought it was fun.

I don't want you to think that the Englishman came too badly out of the affair. Outside the door he had time to think, and his thoughts led him to the telephone in the next flat. He got straight through to me at my flat and woke me out of that deepest middle sleep. That was why when Martins rang up an hour later I already knew what was worrying him. He never said anything bad about policemen after that night.

If the International Patrol made an arrest, they had to take the prisoner to the International Headquarters. This was what the Russian was trying not to do. But I had given my orders to the British policeman.

When he went back to Anna's room there was a quarrel. Anna had told the American that she had Austrian papers (which was true) and that they were

quite in order (which was not quite true). The American told the Russian in bad German that they had no right to arrest an Austrian. He asked Anna for her papers and when she handed them over, the Russian took them from her hand.

"Hungarian," he said, "Hungarian – bad, bad."

The American, whose name was O'Brien, said, "Give the girl back her papers," which the Russian did not understand. The American put his hand on his gun, and the British policeman said, "Let it go, Pat."

"If those papers are not in order we have got a right to look."

"Just let it go. We'll see them at *HQ*."

"If we get to HQ. As like as not he'll drive right through to the Russian zone."

"We'll see," said the British policeman.

They got back into the car with Anna, who sat in front between the two Russians. After they had gone a little way the American touched the Russian on the shoulder. "Wrong way," he said. "HQ that way." The Russian spoke away in his own language while they drove on. "It's what I said," O'Brien told the Englishman. "They are taking her to the Russian zone." Anna stared out in panic. "Don't worry, little girl," O'Brien said. "I'll fix them all right."

The driver stopped suddenly: there was a road *block*. You see, I knew they would have to pass here if they did not make their way to the International HQ. I put my head in at the window and said to the Russian, "What are you doing in the British zone?"

He said it was "orders".

"Whose orders? Let me see them." I noted the

HQ, headquarters.
block, here: soldiers stopping cars and people wanting to go through.

signature. I said, "This tells you to pick up a certain Hungarian woman who is living with false papers in the British zone. Let me see the papers."

He started on a long explanation, but I saw the papers in his pocket, and I pulled them out. He put his hand on his gun, and I hit him in the face, and it made him quiet – that and seeing three British soldiers coming up to the car. I said, "These papers look to me quite in order, but I'll have them gone through and send a report to your colonel. He can, of course, have the lady sent over at any time." I said to Anna, "Get out of the car." She couldn't get by the Russian, so I had to pull him out first. Then I put a packet of cigarettes in his hand and said, "Have a good smoke," waved my hand to the others, and that was the end of that.

---

signature, name signed.

Questions

1. Why did Martins go back to Colonel Calloway?
2. Where had the man disappeared to?
3. What did the porter tell Martins?
4. Why did the International Patrol go to Anna's house?
5. How did they open the door?
6. What was comic about the situation?
7. What did the English soldier do while he was outside the door?
8. Why did Martins never say anything bad about policemen any more?
9. Where were they to take Anna?
10. Why did they not go to Headquarters?
11. Who stopped them?
12. What happened to Anna?

13

While Martins told me how he went back to Anna's and found her gone, I did some hard thinking. I wasn't satisfied with the ghost story, or the idea that the man with Harry Lime's face was only a drunken man's *illusion.* I rang up my assistant and asked him if he knew where Harbin was. He said no. "All right," I said. "Go on trying to get hold of him."

"You know, sir, I can't help feeling that we should have suspected it might be murder. There are one or two points –"

"Put them on paper, Carter."

"Yes, sir. I think, sir, if you don't mind my saying so, we ought to have him dug up. He may not have died just when the others said."

"I agree, Carter."

Martins was right. I had made a fool of myself.

I turned to Martins again and said, "Did you look inside the newspaper kiosk or was it locked?"

"Oh, it wasn't exactly a newspaper kiosk," he said. "It was one of those solid iron kiosks you see everywhere."

"You'd better show me the place."

"But is Anna all right?"

"The police are watching the flat."

I didn't want to frighten people with a police car,

---

illusion, false idea, appearance which is not real.

so we took trams – several trams, and came into the district on foot. "This is the turning," Martins said and led me down a side street. We stopped at the kiosk. "You see, he passed behind here, and disappeared – into the ground."

"That is exactly where he did go," I said.

"How do you mean?"

Martins did not seem to have noticed that the kiosk had a door. I pulled it open and showed him the little iron *staircase* that disappeared into the ground. He said, "Good God, then I didn't imagine him."

"It's one of the entrances to the *main sewer*."

"And anyone can go down?"

"Anyone. For some reason the Russians don't want them locked."

"How far can one go?"

"Right across Vienna. People used them during the war; some people hid there for two years. The Austrians have special police for patrolling these sewers." I closed the door of the kiosk again. I said, "So that's how your friend Harry disappeared."

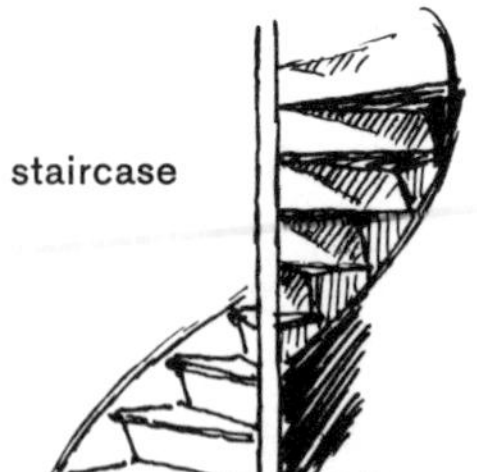

---

main, most important, biggest.

"You really believe it was Harry?"

"Everything points that way."

"Then whom did they bury?"

"I don't know yet, but we soon shall, because we are digging him up again. I've got an idea that Koch was not the only man they murdered."

Martins said, "It's a bit of a shock."

"Yes."

"What are you going to do about it?"

"I don't know."

Martins said, "I wish I could speak to him. You see, there's so much I simply can't believe."

"Perhaps you are the only one who could speak to him. There is a risk, though, because you know too much."

"I still can't believe – I only saw the face for a moment." He said, "What shall I do?"

"He won't leave the Russian zone now. Perhaps that's why he tried to have the girl taken over – because he loves her? I don't know. I do know that the only person who could make him come over would be you – or her, if he still believes you are his friend. But first you've got to speak to him. I can't see how."

"I could go and see Kurtz. I have the address."

I said, "Remember. Lime may not want you to leave the Russian zone once you are there, and I can't help you there."

"I want to clear the whole thing up," Martins said ."I don't want to help you to catch him, but I'll talk to him. That's all."

Questions

1. Why did Carter want to have Harry Lime dug up again?
2. How did they get to the kiosk?
3. What is a sewer?
4. How could Martins meet Lime?

block

14

Martins was careful to carry with him all his papers, also the one that allowed him to move freely through the four zones of Vienna. He had no difficulty in finding Mr Kurtz's *block*, and when he rang the bell the door was opened quickly by Mr Kurtz himself.

"Oh," Mr Kurtz said, "it's you, Mr Martins," and put his hand to the back of his head. Mr Kurtz was not wearing his toupee. Martins had been wondering why he looked so different, and now he knew. Kurtz said, "It would have been better to have telephoned me. You nearly missed me; I was going out."

"May I come in a moment?"

"Of course."

In the hall Martins saw Mr Kurtz's overcoat, his raincoat, a couple of hats and the toupee. He said, "I'm glad to see your hair has grown."

"It keeps the head warm," said Kurtz.

"Whose head?" said Martins, for it had suddenly struck him how useful that toupee might have been on the day of the accident. "Never mind," he went on quickly. "I'm here to see Harry."

"Harry?"

"I want to talk to him."

"Are you mad?"

"I'm in a hurry, so let us suppose that I am. But if you should see Harry – or his ghost – let him know that I want to talk to him. A ghost isn't afraid of a man, is it? Surely it's the other way round. I'll be waiting in the *Prater* by the *Big Wheel* for the next two hours – if you can get in touch with the dead." He added, "Remember I was Harry's friend."

Kurtz said nothing, but somewhere in another room, somebody *cleared his throat*. Martins threw open a door: he had half expected to see the dead rise again, but it was only Dr Winkler who rose from a kitchen chair.

Martins said, "Tell the doctor about my madness. He might be able to tell you all about it. And remember the place – the Great Wheel. Or do ghosts only rise by night?" He left the flat.

For an hour he waited, walking up and down to keep warm. The Prater was nearly empty, a few children were playing and a few young couples entered the cars of the Wheel. Martins wondered who would come for him. Was there enough friendship left in Harry for him to come alone, or would there be a *squad* of police? And then as the hand of his watch passed the hour, he wondered: was it all an illusion? are they digging up Harry's body now in the Central Cemetery?

Somewhere a man was whistling, and Martins knew the tune. He turned and waited. Was it fear that made his heart beat – or just the things which

---

Prater, park in Vienna.
clear one's throat, cough.
squad, group of men.

Big Wheel

that tune called up in his mind, for life had always *quickened* when Harry came, came just as he came now, as though nothing much had happened.

"Harry."

---

quicken, become quicker or more lively.

"Hullo, Rollo."

Harry Lime didn't make the mistake of putting out a hand that Martins might not have taken, but instead he just touched his elbow and said, "How are things?"

"We've got to talk, Harry."

"Of course."

"Alone."

"We couldn't be more alone than here."

He had always known how to do things, and even here he knew, *tipping* the woman in charge of the Wheel, so that they might have a *car* to themselves. He said, "Lovers used to do this in the old days, but they haven't the money now," and he looked out of the window of the car while the city sank very slowly on one side of them.

"Well," Harry said, "it's good to see you, Rollo."

"I was at your funeral."

"That was pretty *smart* of me, wasn't it?"

"Not so smart for your girl. She was there too – in tears."

"She is a good little thing," Harry said. "I'm very fond of her."

"I didn't believe the police when they told me about you," I said. Harry said, "I wouldn't have asked you to come if I'd known what was going to happen, but I didn't think the police were on to me."

"Were you going to share the money with me?"

---

tip, give money to somebody for service rendered.
smart, clever.

car

“I’ve never kept you out of anything, old man, yet.” He stood with his back to the door as the car swung up, and smiled back at Rollo Martins. Martins remembered him as a school boy standing like that and saying, “I’ve learnt a way to get out at night. It’s absolutely safe. You are the only one who I’m going to tell.” Martins thought, “He has never grown up.”

To Harry he said, “Have you ever visited the children’s hospital?”

Harry felt the back of the door with his hand. “Look down there, Rollo,” he said. “Would you really feel any pity if any of those little *dots* stopped moving – for ever? If I said you could have twenty thousand pounds for every dot that stops, would you really, old man, tell me to keep the money?"

"You are finished now. The police know everything."

"But they can't catch me, Rollo, you'll see. I'll come up again. You can't keep a good man down."

The car stopped at the highest point and Harry turned his back and looked out of the window. Martins thought: One good push and I could break the glass, and he imagined the body falling, falling. He said, "You know the police are planning to dig up your body. What will they find?"

"Harbin." He turned away from the window and said, "Look at the sky."

"Why did the Russian try to take Anna?"

"She had false papers, old man."

"Who told them?"

"The price for living in this zone is that you give them a little information now and then."

"She loves you."

"Well, I gave her a good time."

"And I love her."

"That's fine, old man. Be kind to her. And you can help to keep her mouth shut."

"I'd like to knock you through the window."

"But you won't, old man. Kurtz tried to persuade me not to come but I know you. Then he tried to per-

---

dot, little black spot.

suade me to, well, arrange an accident. He told me it would be easy in this car."

"Except that I am the stronger of us."

"But I've got a gun. You don't think they would be able to see what had happened when you hit the ground?" Again the car began to move. "What fools we are, Rollo, talking like this, as if I'd do that to you – or you to me." He turned his back and leaned his face against the glass. "How much do your books give you a year?"

"A thousand."

"And you pay *tax.* I make thirty thousand, free."

"You used to be a Catholic."

"Oh, I still believe. In God and mercy and all that. I'm not hurting anybody's soul by what I do. The dead are happier dead. I could *cut* you *in,* you know. It would be useful. I have no one left in the Inner City."

"Except Cooler? And Winkler?"

"You mustn't *turn* policeman, old man." They left the car and he put his hand again on Martins' elbow. "Have you heard anything of old Bracer?"

"I had a card at Christmas."

"Those were the days, old man. Well, I've got to leave you here. We'll see each other some time. If you are in trouble, you can always get me at Kurtz's." He moved away and turning waved his hand. It was

---

tax, money you pay to the State.
cut in, take in as a member.
turn, become.

like the whole past moving off under a cloud. Martins suddenly called after him. "Don't *trust* me, Harry," but there was too great a distance between them for the words to carry.

Questions

1. What did Martins say to Kurtz?
2. Where did he want to meet Harry?
3. Who was in the other room?
4. Why did Kurtz say that Martins was mad?
5. How long did he have to wait?
6. Where did they go to be alone?
7. What was Lime's view of life?
8. What had Kurtz suggested?
9. What did Martins suddenly think he might do?
10. What did Lime still believe in?
11. What did Martins shout after Lime when he left?

---

trust, have confidence in, believe in.

15

"Anna was at the theatre," Martins told me. "She acted badly – she wasn't much of an actress at the best of times. I saw her afterwards in her dressing-room. I told her Harry was alive – I thought she would be glad, but she sat in front of her mirror and let the tears run down her face. I wished afterwards that she had been glad. She looked awful and I loved her. Then I told her about my interview with Harry, but she did not really listen, and when I'd finished she said, 'I wish he was dead.'

'He *deserves* to be.'

'I mean he would be safe then – from everybody.'"

I asked Martins, "Did you show her the pictures of the children?"

"Yes. I put them up before her and said, 'The police can't arrest Harry unless they get him into this zone, and we've got to help.'

She said, 'I thought he was your friend.' I said, 'He was my friend.' She said, 'I'll never help you to get Harry. I don't want to see him again, I don't want to hear his voice, but I won't do a thing to *harm* him.'"

I said to Martins, "And then?"

Martins said, "Oh, I just got up and left her. Now it's your turn to work on me. What do you want me to do?"

---

deserve, have a right to, be worthy of.
harm, hurt, do wrong.

"I want to act quickly. You see, it was Harbin's body in the coffin, so we can pick up Winkler and Cooler at once. Kurtz is out of our reach, and so is the driver. A message should go from you to Lime at once – not after you have hung around in this zone for twenty-four hours. He should be made to understand that you were brought here as soon as you got back; you heard from me about Harbin; you put two and two together and you go and warn Cooler. He will go and see Kurtz, and Lime will know that you have played the game. Three hours later you send the message that the police are after you and you must see him."

"He won't come."

"I'm not so sure. We'll find a place where we can hide – and where he thinks there is no risk. He would like to know that he *got you out*, and it would stop your mouth."

Martins said, "He never used to get me out at school."

"That wasn't such serious trouble."

He said, "I told Harry not to trust me, but he didn't hear."

"Do you agree?"

"Yes," he said, "I agree."

---

got you out, helped you to escape.

Questions

1. What did Anna do when she heard that Harry was alive?
2. What did Anna say when Martins suggested they should help the police?
3. Whose body was in the coffin?
4. Why was Martins to go and warn Cooler?

16

All the first part went according to plan. We did not arrest Winkler until after Cooler had been warned. Martins enjoyed his short interview with Cooler. "Why, Mr Martins," said Cooler, "it's good to see you. Sit down. I am glad everything went off all right between you and Colonel Calloway."

"It didn't," Martins said.

"You are not angry, I'm sure, that I told him about you seeing Koch. The fact that I liked you should not prevent me from doing my duty."

"Is it a duty to give false evidence at an inquest?"

Cooler said, "Oh, that old story. I'm afraid you a r e angry with me ..."

"The police have dug up the body. They'll be after you and Winkler. I want you to warn Harry ..."

"I don't understand."

"Oh, yes, you do." And it was clear that he did. Martins left him.

I studied a map of the sewer system and came to the conclusion that a café somewhere near the entrance of the great sewer, which was in what Martins had called a newspaper kiosk, would be the best spot. There Lime only had to come up, walk fifty yards, bring Martins back with him, and sink again into the darkness of the sewers. He certainly knew that one patrol of the sewer police ended before midnight, and the next did not start till two, and so at midnight Martins sat in the little cold café near the kiosk, drinking coffee after coffee. I had lent him a revolver; I had men posted as close to the kiosk as I could, and the sewer police were ready. I intended, if I could, to catch Lime before he went underground again. It would save trouble – and risk to Martins. So there in the café Martins sat.

The wind had risen again, but it had brought no snow. There was no heating in the café, and Martins sat warming each hand in turn on a cup of coffee – many cups. There was one of my men with him most of the time, but I changed them every twenty minutes. More than an hour passed. Martins had long given up hope and so had I, where I waited at the phone several streets away, with a party of the sewer police. Suddenly the telephone rang. It was Martins. He said, "I am dying with cold. It's a quarter past one. Is there any point in going on?"

"You shouldn't telephone. You must stay in sight."

Martins' voice said suddenly, "Christ, he's here. He's –" and then the telephone went dead. I said to my assistant, "Give the signal to guard all manholes," and to my sewer police, "We are going down."

What had happened was this. Martins was still on the telephone when Harry Lime came into the café. I don't know what he heard, if he heard anything. Seeing a man speaking on the telephone would have been enough to warn him, if that man was wanted by the police and was without friends in Vienna.

He was out of the café before Martins had put down the receiver. It was one of the rare moments when none of my men was in the café. One had just left and another was outside waiting to go in. Harry Lime ran past him and *made for* the kiosk. Martins came out of the café and saw my men. If he had called out then, it would have been an easy shot, but Martins waited just long enough for Lime to put the kiosk between them: then he called out, "That's him," but Lime was already underground.

What a strange world unknown to most of us lies under our feet. The main sewer, half as wide as the Thames, rushes by under a huge *arch*, fed by smaller streams; these streams have fallen in waterfalls from higher levels and have been *purified* in their fall, so that the air is fresh and the darkness full of the sound of falling and rushing water. The water was just beginning to draw back when Martins and the policeman reached the river: first the staircase, then a short *passage* so low that they had to bend, and then the water flowed round their feet.

My man shone his *torch* along the stream and said, "He has gone that way. Keep behind me, sir, he may shoot."

"Then why should you be in front?"

"It is my job, sir." The water came half-way up their legs as they walked. He took out a whistle and blew, and very far away, here and again there, came the notes of a reply. He said, "They are all down here now. The sewer police, I mean." He lifted his

---

made for, went up to.
purify, make clean.

torch for a moment to shine it ahead, and at that moment the shot came. The torch flew out of his hand and fell in the stream.

"Are you hurt?"

"No, only my hand, that's all. A week off work. Here, sir, take this other torch, while I tie my hand up. Don't shine it. He is in one of the passages." For a long time the sound of the shot went on echoing: when the last echo died away a whistle blew ahead of them, and the policeman blew an answer.

Martins said, "It's a strange thing – I don't even know your name."

"Bates, sir."

Martins said, "Let me come in front. I don't think he'll shoot at me, and I want to talk to him."

"I had orders to look after you, sir. Be careful."

"That's all right."

He went round Bates and called out, "Harry," and the name sent up an echo, "Harry, Harry, Harry!"

A voice came out quite near, "Is that you old man? What do you want me to do?"

"Come out. And put your hands above your head."

"I haven't a torch. I can't see a thing."

"Be careful, sir," said Bates.

"Get flat against the wall. He won't shoot at me," Martins said. He called, "Harry, I'm going to shine the torch. Come out. You haven't got a chance."

He shone the torch, and twenty feet away, Harry came out. "Hands above the head, Harry." Harry raised his hands and fired and Martins heard Bates cry out. At the same moment a strong light lit the whole place. My party had reached the scene. Lime turned this way and that, he couldn't see a thing; then suddenly he jumped into the water which took him past the body of Bates into the dark. Martins stood half in darkness. He had his gun in his hand. "There," I said. "There. Shoot." He lifted the gun and fired. "Well done," I called and stopped at Bates' body. He was dead. I looked up and Martins was out of sight. Then I heard a third shot.

Martins told me later, "I walked up the stream to find Harry, but I must have missed him in the dark. I was afraid to lift the torch: I didn't want him to

shoot again. He must have been hit just at the entrance of a side passage. Then I suppose he must have *crawled* up the passage to the foot of the iron stairs. Thirty feet above his head was the manhole, but he wouldn't have been strong enough to lift it, and even if he had, the police would have been waiting for him. He began to pull himself up the stairs, but couldn't go on. What made him whistle the tune I'd been fool enough to believe he had written himself, I don't know. But I heard it, and found my way up to where he lay. "Harry," I said, and the whistling stopped, just above my head. I put my hand on the iron staircase and began to go up. Then, only three steps up, my foot touched his hand, and he was there. I shone my torch on him; he hadn't got

---

crawl, move on one's hands and knees.

a gun. For a moment I thought he was dead. I said, "Harry," and he turned his eyes to my face. He was trying to speak, and I bent down to listen. "Fool", he said. I don't know if he meant that for himself – or for me. Then he began to *whimper* again. I couldn't bear it any more and I lifted my gun and fired."

"We'll forget that bit," I said.

Martins said, "I never shall."

---

whimper, cry like a small, sick child.

Questions

1 What did Martins say to Cooler?
2. Where was Martins to wait for Harry Lime?
3. Who was to be with him?
4. What was the weather like?
5. What happened when he was speaking on the telephone?
6. What did Lime do when he saw Martins at the telephone?
7. Why did the torch fall out of Bates' hand?
8. Why did Martins wish to be in front?
9. What happened to Bates?
10. What did Harry do when he raised his hands above his head?
11. Where had Martins gone?
12. Where did he find Lime?
13. What did he do when he saw that Lime was dying?
14. Why did Calloway not want him to say the last words?

17

A *thaw* had set in, and all over Vienna the snow melted. Electric drills were no longer needed to break the frozen ground. It was almost as warm as a spring day when Harry Lime had his second funeral. I was glad to get him under earth again, but it had taken two men's deaths. The group by the grave was smaller now – only the girl, and Rollo Martins and myself.

After it was over the girl walked away without a word to either of us. I said to Martins, "I've got transport. Can I give you a lift?"

"No," he said, "I'll take the tram back."

"You win, you've proved me to be a fool."

"I haven't won," he said. "I've lost." I watched him walking after the girl. He caught her up and they walked side by side. I don't think he said a word to her: it was like the end of a story, except that before they turned out of my sight her hand was through his arm – which is how a story usually begins. He was a very bad shot, but he had a way with Westerns – and with girls. And Crabbin? Oh, Crabbin is still trying to make somebody pay Dexter's expenses. They say they can't pay at the same time in Stockholm and Vienna. Poor Crabbin. Poor all of us, when you come to think of it.

---

thaw, melting of snow.

Questions

1. Why was it easier to dig a grave for Harry the second time?

2. Why did Martins want to take the tram back?

3. In what way was the end of the story like a beginning?